# WHAT WOULD
# HARRY DO?

## LESSONS FOR LIVING LIKE A HERO FROM
## THE WIZARDING WORLD OF HARRY POTTER

JULIANA SHARAF

*Harry Potter and the Sorcerer's Stone* (2001). According to *wizardingworld.com*, production designer Stuart Craig revealed that the model of Hogwarts measured 80 feet in diameter.

# It All Started With a Book

**N**early three decades after *Harry Potter and the Sorcerer's Stone* launched an international phenomenon, it's clear the series's magic has only become more potent with time. Those of us who grew up alongside the Boy Who Lived—who can recall the joy of midnight release parties and the crazed feeling of waiting years for a book only to devour it in a matter of hours—know the story's staying power is part of what makes it so beloved. There are limitless lessons to be gleaned from the books and their film adaptations. No one book could hope to distill the sagacity delivered as Harry discovers he's a wizard (and defeats one of the world's most powerful), but if the series taught me anything, it's that there's value in giving it your all. No matter how old you were when you first decided the proud, stuffy Dursleys were worth reading about (if only to watch them squirm), I hope the pearls of wisdom hand-picked in these pages will inspire you to return to Harry's story with the same sense of wonder you had the first time you visited Hogwarts.

Rupert Grint, Emma Watson and Daniel Radcliffe in *Harry Potter and the Goblet of Fire* (2005). Between scenes, the actors completed three to five hours of tutoring a day.

# When in Doubt, Go to the Library

**There's no limit to how practical paper-based knowledge can be as long as you remember to use it.**

It takes a humble person to admit how much they don't know; it takes a clever person to know where to start looking. Whenever the trio has a problem to solve, they rarely ask adults for help. Instead, Hermione often leads them to the library ("Because that's what Hermione does..."), where they engage with the silent, impartial wisdom provided by books. From learning about Nicolas Flamel in *Sorcerer's Stone* to discovering horrifying details about basilisks in *Chamber of Secrets* to poring over ways to survive underwater in *Goblet of Fire,* Harry and his friends make a habit of tearing through the most instructive wizarding titles they can get their hands on. Unlike Muggles, they have no internet access to speak of, and they're better off for it.

One of the benefits of consulting paper-based knowledge is you can do so discreetly, which is helpful when your school is being governed by a sadistic tyrant bent on breaking your spirit. It's telling that in *Order of the Phoenix*, when Harry hosts Dumbledore's Army meetings out of the Room of Requirement, the Room offers bookcases packed with tomes on advanced defensive spellwork. And, at least until Umbridge is made aware of the Room, these books remain a closely guarded secret known only to those who need them most.

Margin notes, such as the ones Harry studies in *Half-Blood Prince*, act as portals of discovery, connecting us with the inner musings of readers who lived decades or centuries before we turned the cover. If you're lucky enough to have a non-Euclidean bag like Hermione's charmed accessory in *Deathly Hallows*, you can pack an unlimited reading supply without a single thought to the laws of physics.

Take a note from the trio: Whatever life throws at you, you can always turn to a book for guidance. Even if it tries to bite your hand off.

**Emma Watson as Hermione Granger in *Harry Potter and the Sorcerer's Stone* (2001). Watson auditioned for the role a grueling eight times before securing the part.**

Daniel Radcliffe and John Cleese in *Harry Potter and the Chamber of Secrets* (2002). Cleese is one of a number of Oscar nominees in the film, in addition to Kenneth Branagh, Richard Harris Maggie Smith and Julie Walters.

# Choose Your Words Wisely

*"Once again, you show all the sensitivity of a blunt axe."*
—Nearly Headless Nick, *Harry Potter and the Half-Blood Prince*

For someone who died ages ago, you'd think a ghost like Nick would be less touchy about the fact that he's not alive. But when Ron makes a bold observation to that end in *Half-Blood Prince*, Nick utters the line above, then glides away in a huff. After all, had it not been for Nick's poor spellwork in 1492, he wouldn't have botched his attempt at beautifying a noble, an event that prompted his execution (which itself went poorly). Proud to a fault, the former Sir Nicholas de Mimsy-Porpington proves that even ghosts have feelings. There's no telling when a brazen comment, joke or piece of ill-timed advice might be the thing that derails someone's day or week (or afterlife), even when you're stating the obvious. Unless you aim to offend, weigh your words carefully. You don't want your friends to (nearly) lose their heads over something you meant only in passing.

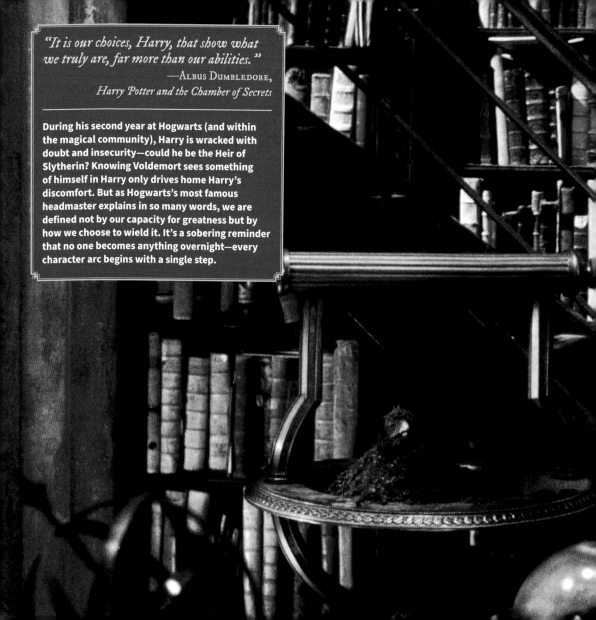

> *"It is our choices, Harry, that show what we truly are, far more than our abilities."*
>
> —ALBUS DUMBLEDORE,
> *Harry Potter and the Chamber of Secrets*

During his second year at Hogwarts (and within the magical community), Harry is wracked with doubt and insecurity—could he be the Heir of Slytherin? Knowing Voldemort sees something of himself in Harry only drives home Harry's discomfort. But as Hogwarts's most famous headmaster explains in so many words, we are defined not by our capacity for greatness but by how we choose to wield it. It's a sobering reminder that no one becomes anything overnight—every character arc begins with a single step.

Richard Harris as Albus
Dumbledore and Daniel
Radcliffe as Harry Potter
in *Harry Potter and the
Chamber of Secrets* (2002).

Tom Felton as Draco Malfoy in a promotional portrait for *Harry Potter and the Sorcerer's Stone* (2001). Before landing the role, Felton auditioned to play Harry and Ron.

# Mind the Company You Keep

*"You don't want to go making friends with the wrong sort."*
—Draco Malfoy, *Harry Potter and the Sorcerer's Stone*

rrogant, petty and entitled to a fault, Draco is the quintessential Slytherin student of Harry's class, constantly looking out for himself and his fellow dungeon-dwellers at the expense of others. The only child of Narcissa and Lucius Malfoy—a Voldemort sympathizer and Death Eater, respectively—Draco knows the prestige and protection afforded by mingling with a certain crowd. It's an association that will haunt him for decades to come. But when he's introduced in *Sorcerer's Stone*, 11-year-old Draco is keen on making friends, much like Harry. In a moment brimming with irony, he extends some well-intentioned advice to the classmate he'll come to view as his archenemy. And while Draco misses the fact that this warning outs him as the "sort" of person Harry won't tolerate, he isn't wrong: Our inner circle is an outward reflection of our values. All the more reason to mind the company we keep.

Fawkes the phoenix on display at Harry Potter: The Exhibition in Madrid, Spain, in 2017. The Spanish leg of the European tour ran from November 18, 2017, through April 2, 2018.

# Be a Phoenix

When it comes to reinventing ourselves, Muggles can learn a lot from these mythical birds that are no strangers to living, dying and living again.

It's difficult enough to grasp the finality of death, a thought that likely horrifies Harry when he witnesses Dumbledore's phoenix, Fawkes, burst into flames in the headmaster's office. Though he looks around for water to douse the animal, it's too late to save "the decrepit-looking bird that resembled a half-plucked turkey" from his incendiary demise. Dumbledore enters and reassures Harry his phoenix is not gone for good—he merely reached the end of a life cycle. Moments later, Harry spots a tiny chick emerging from the smoldering ashes lining Fawkes's cage. All is not lost, despite how stark the pyrotechnics might have looked.

By the time Harry faces off against the basilisk in the Chamber of Secrets later that school year, Fawkes is strong enough to bring him the Sorting Hat, slash the basilisk's eyes, heal Harry's mortal wound with his tears and even carry Harry and several others out of the depths of the Chamber, none of which he could've possibly accomplished prior to Harry's arrival in Dumbledore's office that day. Like the rest of his species, Fawkes has mastered the art of beginning again, especially when all signs point to the end. Dumbledore even confides in Harry how Fawkes had put off his "Burning Day" for days, to the point the headmaster's been telling his beloved companion to "get a move on."

When you feel a path you've chosen has reached its conclusion— whether that's a job, a relationship or a hobby that no longer excites or challenges you—it can be tempting to put off ending what you've stuck with for so long. But in doing so, we miss the chance to reinvent ourselves, to live fully as we cycle through life's seasons.

Dumbledore (Richard M...

Rupert Grint, Daniel Radcliffe, Julie Walters, Mark Williams and James and Oliver Phelps in *Harry Potter and the Chamber of Secrets* (2002). The kitchen of the Weasley family home, the Burrow, can be seen on the Warner Brothers Harry Potter studio tour in London.

# Stay Curious

Soon after Harry flees the trappings of the Muggle world for his first return to Hogwarts, he meets his best friend's father, Arthur Weasley, who asks him the question above. Arthur makes a living at the Ministry of Magic by altering the memories of non-magical people who've encountered cursed magical objects. Though it barely pays the bills, he couldn't be happier. Much like an archaeologist is keen to uncover the purpose of an artifact whose use escapes them, Arthur is mystified by all things made by those who live without magical means. His undying zeal to explore the machinations of Muggles is on par with Harry's hunger to prove he belongs in the magical community. Arthur, whose joy for discovery and all-consuming need to decipher life's unknowns uplifts those around him, exemplifies the spirit of the lifelong learner. The Weasley patriarch shows that choosing to look at old things with new eyes every day is nothing short of magical.

James Phelps, Rupert Grint, Chris Rankin, Emma Watson, Julie Walters and George Harris in *Harry Potter and the Deathly Hallows: Part 2* (2011).

*"Every human life is worth the same, and worth saving."*
—Kingsley Shacklebolt, *Harry Potter and the Deathly Hallows*

At Harry's most desperate hour hunting Horcruxes in the final *Potter* installment, it's no small consolation when he hears familiar voices on the underground radio program *Potterwatch*. Among them, Auror Kingsley Shacklebolt, who urges listeners to rail against anti-Muggle hate crimes committed by Death Eaters and Voldemort sympathizers. If one group of people can be made the enemy, it's a slippery slope until others are caught in the ever-widening net of persecution. When times are tough, heed the call for collectivism and look out for others.

A scene from *Harry Potter and the Sorcerer's Stone* (2001). This was the only film in the series to use real flames in the Great Hall floating candle scenes—due to safety concerns, CGI achieved the effect in subsequent installments.

# Good Food Brings People Together

Nothing ensnares the senses, as Professor Snape would put it, quite like tucking into a satisfying meal with equally appetizing company.

A delicious dish appeals to people from all walks of life, and one of the enduring joys of the *Harry Potter* series is the attention and care paid to the moments in which characters enjoy a hot meal together.

It's no accident that every school year at Hogwarts opens just after the Sorting Ceremony with a feast, where students get to know their new Housemates over steaming plates of roast beef, shepherd's pie, mashed potatoes, fried tomatoes and more. Regional foods like bouillabaisse, chocolate éclairs and goulash, offered when

Hogwarts hosts international students as part of the Triwizard Tournament in *Goblet of Fire*, make guests feel at home and provide people like Harry with glimpses of places they've never been. These feasts regularly reunite students and teachers for various holidays (especially meaningful for those who have nowhere to go on Christmas) and it's how Hogwarts ends each year on a sweet note.

Harry's also treated to other culinary delights while dining at the Burrow, the Weasley family abode. Chatting between bites of chicken and ham pie, corned beef sandwiches and humble breakfast staples like marmalade on toast, the Weasley clan makes Harry feel like he's one of the family, welcoming the Boy Who Lived like one of their own.

Whether he's enjoying **Chocolate Frogs** or the risky but rewarding Bertie Bott's Every Flavor Beans, nearly every bit of food Harry encounters is served alongside a meaningful conversation, a moment of revelation or a sop for the soul. Gathering your favorite people around the table for a bite can be a magical experience and is one of the few rituals we have in common. Just as quality food sustains our bodies, the company of friends and family can nourish our spirit. The wandless spellwork of whipping up a feast for those closest to us—even if your only specialty is a slightly burnt grilled cheese sandwich—isn't limited to elves or wizards, and it certainly won't break the Statute of Secrecy.

Alan Rickman as
Severus Snape in
*Harry Potter and the
Deathly Hallows: Part 1*
(2010). While Rickman
had always been the
author's preferred
actor for the Potions
professor, studio
executives first favored
Tim Roth for the role.

# Know Your Goals and Follow Through on Them

*"Everything was supposed to be to keep Lily Potter's son safe."*
—Severus Snape, *Harry Potter and the Deathly Hallows*

As Albus Dumbledore's double agent, former Death Eater Severus Snape has a lot on his plate. He spies on the most powerful Dark wizard of all time while keeping careless, hot-headed young wizards from blowing themselves up as he instructs them in the art of potion-making—all to protect the son of his worst bully who, as it so happens, married Snape's only love. But spurred by his ceaseless guilt for sealing Lily Potter's fate, Snape can steel himself through just about any challenge, even when it means looking out for an ungrateful, reckless (and occasionally hateful) teen.

Your goals may not include taking down a sociopathic mass murderer, but take it from Snape: the success of any plan starts with your will to execute it. When you know what you have to do, the objectives fall into place. All that's left is to shut your mind to the noise and see them through.

THE DAILY PROPHET COMPETITION
WIN A NIGHT IN
TRANSYLVANIA

DAILY P
THE WIZARD WORLDS PROCLIM

National Weather
Zodiac ★ Aspec

EXCLUSIVE
THE BOY WHO

*"It is the quality of one's convictions that determines success, not the number of followers."*

—Remus Lupin,
*Harry Potter and the Deathly Hallows: Part 2* (2011)

As a werewolf, Lupin is no stranger to living as a loner. But as we know by the last *Potter* installment, he's built a life with Nymphadora Tonks and become a father. As Hogwarts prepares for the final showdown with Voldemort, Lupin stares down the oncoming horde of Death Eaters and offers the above line, ready to give his all for the cause. No matter how bleak things might be, take a note from Lupin and revel in knowing you've fought for what's right.

Harry Taylor and Daniel Radcliffe in *Harry Potter and the Sorcerer's Stone* (2001). Hedwig, Harry's feathered companion, is never referenced by name throughout the first film of the series.

# Venture Into Parts Unknown

Leaving everything we know behind—whether for a weekend or for good—has meaningful benefits beyond the change of scenery.

W hen we encounter Harry in *Sorcerer's Stone*, his day-to-day existence consists of receiving constant insults from his aunt and uncle or steering clear of his cousin Dudley, who enjoys treating him like a punching bag. Harry is rarely invited to join his relatives when they pursue something entertaining. And when he does come along, it's under the scrutiny and watchful eye of Uncle Vernon.

Rubeus Hagrid, the half-giant who breaks down a door to retrieve the Boy Who Lived from the Dursleys, gives Harry his first taste of freedom (as well as birthdae cake). It's a thrill anyone can appreciate, whether you first left your hometown at the tender age of 11 or 111. The act of leaving the world he knows is the one that first sets Harry on his journey to becoming a wizard. For the first time, Harry can go where he wants and do as he pleases, and after making a stop at Gringotts, he even has ample gold to spend however he likes (And what greater freedom is there than financial independence?). Well before he enters the Great Hall or boards the Hogwarts Express, he discovers the magical world in all its strange glory, entering an entirely new society that's been waiting to embrace him his whole life.

Whether you find the means to go it alone or are lucky enough to have a friend or two for company, stepping beyond the world you're accustomed to is sure to change your perspective in ways you can hardly imagine. While you may not find yourself in a flying car or riding a Thestral, there will almost assuredly be cake. Don't be afraid to take a bite.

**Tom Felton as Draco Malfoy in *Harry Potter and the Chamber of Secrets* (2002). Felton's skateboarding on set prompted the studio to enact a curfew on potentially dangerous pastimes.**

# Learn to Improvise

*"I didn't know you could read."*
—Draco Malfoy, *Harry Potter and the Chamber of Secrets* (2002)

When the film adaptation of *Chamber of Secrets* hit theaters in 2002, viewers couldn't have known one of the most iconic Draco digs of the series was not the work of screenwriters taking liberties with the source material. In fact, the above quip only came about as the result of Tom Felton forgetting his line. Granted, mistakes happen, even for seasoned professionals. But what sets the pros and amateurs apart is how they respond to chaos, whether external or (as in the case of a dropped line) self-inflicted.

Diverting from the plan—from any one project or, in a greater sense, the script of what you've imagined for yourself—doesn't have to end with beating yourself up or obsessively replaying the blooper reel of your life. Sometimes, it's a chance to generate something greater than what was there at the start. What you might initially regard as an error could be a chance to showcase your genius.

Geraldine Somerville, Daniel Radcliffe and Adrian Rawlins in *Harry Potter and the Sorcerer's Stone* (2001). Radcliffe made his film debut earlier that year in *The Tailor of Panama* (2001).

# Your Public Perception Does Not Define You

You can't control what others think of you—only the way you carry yourself.

Long before the Boy Who Lived set foot in the Great Hall, the magical community knew Harry as the child the Dark Lord failed to kill—the infant who stripped Voldemort of his corporeal form and ended a war. Harry knows he wasn't actively responsible for Voldemort's destruction. Only later did he learn his mother's love made it possible. But this miraculous survival story marks him as a celebrity. It's a cross to bear that most people take for a crown, and from the moment he first holds a wand, Hogwarts's students (as well as many members of the faculty) begin sizing up Harry-the-Preteen against Harry-the-Hero.

Even after Harry gets Sorted into Gryffindor, proves himself on the Quidditch pitch and prevents Voldemort from snatching the Sorcerer's Stone there are still doubts. When a basilisk stalks Hogwarts's halls, his classmates wonder: Is Harry the Heir of Slytherin? His selfless good deeds—slaying the monster in the Chamber of Secrets, saving Ginny Weasley—are all but forgotten when his name emerges from the Goblet of Fire. Rumors and sour feelings abound: The underage wizard must have entered a competition with a shocking mortality rate for fun. And when Harry—clinging to Cedric Diggory's corpse as proof—insists Voldemort has staged a comeback, the Ministry of Magic brands him a liar. According to the court of public opinion, he might as well be a Slytherin.

If there's one thing a Patronus won't drive off, it's gossip. It's a good thing Harry never puts much stock in being liked; otherwise, he would've never found the time to hunt Horcruxes.

Harry never lets rumors sway him from his values, and neither should you. Ignore the naysayers and let your work speak for itself.

**Maggie Smith and Daniel Radcliffe in** *Harry Potter and the Sorcerer's Stone* **(2001). In 2003, Smith completed the triple crown of acting —winning an Academy Award, Emmy Award and Tony Award—when she took home an Emmy for her starring role in HBO's television movie** *My House in Umbria* **(2003).**

> *"Never trust anything that can think for itself if you can't see where it keeps its brain."*
>
> —ARTHUR WEASLEY,
> *Harry Potter and the Chamber of Secrets*

When the Weasley patriarch chides his youngest, Ginny, for writing in a cursed diary, he offers the practical advice above. Given he's a cursed object specialist, Arthur knows to use caution when interacting with something whose design or designs you don't fully comprehend. In the Muggle world, the equivalent of cursed objects is bad intentions, and Arthur's advice applies just the same: If you can't discern precisely what someone wants, it's usually best not to open up until you can.

Julie Walters as Molly Weasley and Mark Williams as Arthur Weasley in *Harry Potter and the Chamber of Secrets* (2002).

Imelda Staunton as Dolores Umbridge in *Harry Potter and the Order of the Phoenix* (2007). Costume designer Jany Temime dressed Staunton in progressively darker shades of pink over the course of the film as the character grows more hysterical.

# Question Authority

People who crave power—including public servants—don't always desire to serve the public. When that happens, it's on you to call them out.

A s children, we're taught that people in power got their roles by virtue of merit, display sound judgment and act with our best interests in mind. Dolores Umbridge, an egotistical bureaucrat with a sadistic streak, proves otherwise. It is not, she shows us, always wise to blindly obey our elders.

In some ways, she outclasses Voldemort with her sheer malicious intent: Like many compelling villains, Umbridge is convinced not only that she's one of the good guys but also that she's meant to use her authority to proselytize her views. Whereas the Dark Lord makes no efforts to conceal his intentions, the Ministry of Magic official cloaks herself under a girlish guise of pink frills and bows, hiding in plain sight—a cowardly act of subterfuge. It's easy to tell that the dark-robed man with dead eyes and a snake nose must be opposed. Umbridge's brand of evil is harder to spot and unfortunately far more common: She is every punishment-obsessed teacher who delights in making an example of a student, every agent of power who values secrecy above transparency.

Umbridge needs no Horcruxes to preserve and magnify her might—she's got bureaucracy for that. Her combination of ignorance, arrogance and authority makes it especially important that our heroes question and oppose her unjust methods and their reasoning. Ultimately, she only wields as much power as the Ministry grants her.

Growing up with an abusive aunt and uncle shaped Harry's distrust of authority, and as a teenager, he knows those who hold power don't always deserve it. You will undoubtedly come across people who abuse their positions, who put their agendas before their responsibilities and who create laws to constrict rather than protect those under their care. When confronted by the Umbridges of the world, your job is to steady yourself and shout *Riddikulus*.

Katie Leung, Tom Felton, Imelda Staunton and David Bradley in *Harry Potter and the Order of the Phoenix* (2007). One of Staunton's neighbors in West Hampstead, London, is fellow *Potter* castmate Emma Thompson (aka Professor Sybill Trelawney).

Evanna Lynch as Luna Lovegood in *Harry Potter and the Order of the Phoenix* (2007). In 2017, Lynch co-founded *The ChickPeeps*, an award-winning podcast about veganism.

# Regrouping Is Not Retreating

*"I think I'll just go down and have some pudding and wait for it all to turn up—it always does in the end."*
—LUNA LOVEGOOD, *Harry Potter and the Order of the Phoenix* (2007)

Not every action requires an immediate response. This is lost on Gryffindors like Harry, whose knack for "daring, nerve, and chivalry" highlights a propensity for jumping into action. But with Voldemort rallying his forces and a sadistic Ministry official on a power trip at Hogwarts, Harry's pushed to his limits—he rushes into battle and gets his godfather killed. Enter Luna Lovegood, who shows that self-preservation begins with conserving one's energy. When Harry learns classmates have been hiding Luna's belongings, he wants to stand up for his friend and make things right. Luna, however, refuses to let the bullying put a damper on the last night of the school year. It's not worth missing a Hogwarts feast. Weathering life's storms takes stamina, so pick your battles and prioritize your needs. That includes keeping your blood sugar up. Find your pudding and savor every bite. You'll need it for the fight to come.

Gary Oldman as Sirius Black in *Harry Potter and the Prisoner of Azkaban* (2004). Prior to accepting the role, Oldman had taken a year off from acting to spend time with family.

# You Don't Always Have the Full Story

Snap judgments can ruin lives. A willingness to listen can save them.

A single fact is little more than a data point. String two or more facts together, though, and you begin to construct a narrative. Make it compelling enough and people won't think twice about believing it, no matter how far it might be from the truth. Such is the case when Harry's godfather, Sirius Black, is accused of murdering James and Lily Potter.

After all, Muggle eyewitnesses claimed he blew up the street—he was found laughing at the scene of the crime, and all that was left of Peter Pettigrew was a finger. It's enough to get him sentenced to Azkaban, where he suffers for 12 nightmarish years before breaking free. Presumably, he's out casing Hogwarts, bent on finishing off his best friend's son. It's only when Harry encounters Sirius in the Shrieking Shack that he hears the unabridged context of that fateful day: Sirius was framed.

Had Harry chosen that moment to eliminate his godfather, he would've either never learned the truth (thinking he'd protected his friends from a maniac) or come to discover he killed an innocent man. No one's told him to think Sirius is anything but guilty. But rather than blindly follow that line of thinking, Harry takes a moment to let Sirius speak for himself, a pause that makes all the difference.

Sirius's plight shows you are far less likely to regret taking the time to hear someone out than casting judgment without all the facts. There could be far more at stake than you realize.

Emma Watson, Daniel Radcliffe, Rupert Grint, David Thewlis and Gary Oldman in *Harry Potter and the Prisoner of Azkaban* (2004). At the press conference for *Harry Potter and the Deathly Hallows: Part 2* (2011), Thewlis named the Marauder's Map as his favorite prop of the series.

*"But you know, happiness can be found even in the darkest of times, if one only remembers to turn on the light."*

—ALBUS DUMBLEDORE,
*Harry Potter and the Prisoner of Azkaban* (2004)

---

**Dumbledore has a knack for dispensing sage advice, and at about 113 years old, he's picked up quite a bit along the way. In a year when Dementors roam the Hogwarts grounds, one must be ready to dispel their all-consuming despair at a moment's notice by focusing on joyful memories. Mostly, he reminds us that happiness is a deliberate act. Be prepared to banish your own intrusive or depressive thoughts by calling on the memories that sustain you.**

# Get to the Point

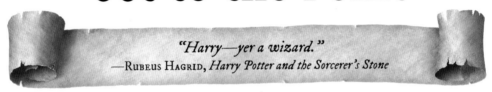

*"Harry—yer a wizard."*
—Rubeus Hagrid, *Harry Potter and the Sorcerer's Stone*

B revity, as the most famous Muggle playwright put it, is the soul of wit. When Hagrid comes to whisk Harry away on his 11th birthday, there's a lot to fill Harry in on: how his parents died, how he got that scar and how it turns out there's an entire society of magic folk that's existed just out of sight and they've sent him gobs of unchecked mail. But rather than throw the Boy Who Lived down a rabbit hole of backstory by subjecting him to a labyrinthine monologue, he gets to the heart of Harry's destiny in less than a handful of words. It's one of Hagrid's most brilliant moments of the series, and the message is simple: When you've got a lot to say, don't bury the lede. Start by cutting to the chase.

Daniel Radcliffe and David Thewlis in *Harry Potter and the Prisoner of Azkaban* (2004). In 2008, Thewlis won the Richard Harris Award for Outstanding Contribution by an Actor at the British Independent Film Awards.

# There's No Teacher Like Experience

## Learning knowledge in theory doesn't hold a candle to relying on it in real-time.

I t's one thing to learn something in a controlled environment, but it's another thing entirely to apply that knowledge in a real-world setting, especially when it comes to warding off soul-sucking wraiths. No one understands this better than Remus Lupin, Harry's third Defense Against the Dark Arts professor. Teaching Harry to use the Patronus Charm goes smoothly (granted, Harry catches on to this spell quicker than most), but to ensure the lesson will stick, Lupin recreates the harrowing experience of encountering a Dementor by having Harry practice the spell on a boggart. Thanks to these lessons, Harry goes on to save lives (including his own), passing the skills he's learned to his peers as part of Dumbledore's Army (who in turn put them to practical use as part of their first fight with real stakes: the harrowing Battle of the Department of Mysteries).

Any teacher worth their salt knows this immersive approach lays the groundwork for internalizing knowledge (as any foreign language student who's studied abroad can attest). There's only so much in-classroom instruction will buy you when it comes to building the muscle memory resulting from converting the theoretical into the practical. When books have yielded all their secrets, it's time to up the ante and hit the field (if only to write your own books in turn, or at least scribble your findings in the margins). Knowledge is power, but only if you put it to use.

David Thewlis as Remus Lupin in *Harry Potter and the Prisoner of Azkaban* (2004). In 2018, Thewlis was nominated for a Golden Globe Award for his role in the third season of *Fargo*.

Rupert Grint as Ron
Weasley and Emma
Watson as Hermione
Granger in *Harry Potter
and the Sorcerer's Stone*
(2001). Watson is also
a certified yoga and
meditation instructor.

# Test Your Limits Responsibly

> *"'Are you sure that's a real spell?' said the girl.*
> *'Well, it's not very good, is it?'"*
> —HERMIONE GRANGER, *Harry Potter and the Sorcerer's Stone*

You don't need a Care of Magical Creatures textbook to know adolescents will test their limits. On the trio's first trip aboard the Hogwarts Express, Ron utters rhyming nonsense in an attempt to turn his rat Scabbers yellow. None of them has yet grasped the consequences of shoddy spellwork, yet nothing happens, so no harm no foul. But when Harry uses a heated moment in his sixth year to employ a curse "for enemies" about which he reads in the margins of a textbook, it's horrifying to see just how devastating getting in over your head can be. Without Snape's quick intervention, *Sectumsempra* would've made Harry a murderer. Taking calculated risks requires understanding what the risks are. When reaching for the unknown, try to keep at least one foot grounded in certainty. Because if anything goes awry, the consequences are manageable rather than irreversible.

Daniel Radcliffe, Devon Murray, Rupert Grint and Emma Watson in *Harry Potter and the Sorcerer's Stone* (2001). As part of his audition for the role of Ron, Grint performed a rap explaining why he wanted the part.

# Stay Humble

### Hear the know-it-all out. You might just learn something.

Few people enjoy being a novice: It's a long slog to mastery, often fraught with repetition, failure and repeated failure. That's not even taking into account the personal hell of group projects, a torture known to wizards and Muggles alike. Acquiring knowledge requires humbling yourself, something Ron is not in the mood to do during a Charms lesson two months into his first year. Paired up with resident know-it-all Hermione, Ron's poor mood sours as she lectures him on how he's been placing the emphasis on the wrong syllable—"it's LeviOsa, not LevioSA"—then impresses Professor Flitwick with her flawless execution of the spell. Ron, for his part, can barely make a feather levitate.

Perhaps on a better day, Ron could've marveled at Hermione's capacity for memory and eagerness to help. He might have even laughed at how close he'd been to getting it right—how if he'd just had a bit more patience, he would've pulled it off. Instead, after class, he calls Hermione a "nightmare" and she hurries off to cry in a bathroom, where she is cornered by an escaped troll. Ironically, Hermione's rescue hinges on how Ron blurts out *Wingardium Leviosa* to knock out the troll with its own club. He might've only heard her say it once, but the moment is seared into his memory, the first thing that comes to his head. It's quite possibly the most effective lesson of his schooling.

Some days you might be Hermione, confident in your abilities, and other days, you're Ron, annoyed, insecure and more than a little jealous. When it's the latter, remind yourself: Take the help you're given. There's no telling how soon you might need it.

Emma Watson as Hermione Granger in *Harry Potter and the Sorcerer's Stone* (2001). As far as her real-life studies are concerned, in 2014, Watson graduated from Brown University with a bachelor's degree in English literature.

Sirius feels a great deal of contempt for Barty Crouch Sr., the Ministry of Magic official who sent him to Azkaban without a trial—a breach of justice and a de facto death sentence. When Hermione expresses her outrage over Crouch Sr.'s mistreatment of his devoted house-elf at the Quidditch World Cup, Sirius tells her she's "got the measure of [him]" down pat. Little does Crouch Sr. seem to mind his actions mirror those of Voldemort, the enemy. No matter your proclaimed values, your deeds will out your true nature in time.

**Gary Oldman as Sirius Black in** *Harry Potter and the Order of the Phoenix* **(2007).**

Daniel Radcliffe and Emma Watson in *Harry Potter and the Order of the Phoenix* (2007). That year, Radcliffe starred in *December Boys* and the television movie *My Boy Jack*.

# Show Up

**You'll never know what opportunities you might miss out on by staying home.**

The pull to stay with the familiar rather than push one's boundaries makes for a remarkably potent veela's song. In a year when he's the subject of a government smear campaign and a sadistic new headmaster enacts a reign of terror at Hogwarts, no one would begrudge Harry for wanting to keep his head down. Well, no one except Hermione, who views Harry as the perfect (and only) option for a competent Defense Against the Dark Arts teacher in a year when Professor Dolores Umbridge would rather they sit quietly and read about defensive spellwork. Like any good friend, she convinces him to go to a seedy bar, where she's arranged for him to meet "a couple" of folks interested in learning what he has to offer. To his shock, 25 people show up. Together, they form the greatest study group in the history of Hogwarts, whose members later hold their own against Death Eaters thanks to Harry's tutelage and encouragement.

The founding of Dumbledore's Army (D.A.) owes everything to the fact that Harry could've just as easily taken one look at the "accumulated filth of centuries" lining the floors of the Hog's Head Inn and strolled off to enjoy a butterbeer in peace at the Three Broomsticks. Instead, he sits with the discomfort of recounting how he witnessed a classmate's murder with the crowd, earning their respect and trust. Even when cruel and unusual punishments are on the line, he leads the D.A. in defensive spellwork training, meeting in secret to hone their skills—all of which only came together because he was vulnerable enough to share his story.

The lesson: Put yourself out there. You might make an ally or 25 along the way. You might even save the world.

Emma Watson, Daniel Radcliffe, Bonnie Wright, Rupert Grint and Matthew Lewis in *Harry Potter and the Order of the Phoenix* (2007). At GalaxyCon Richmond in 2020, Lewis revealed he'd taken the Pottermore Sorting quiz and is, in fact, a Hufflepuff.

Richard Harris as Albus Dumbledore in *Harry Potter and the Sorcerer's Stone* (2001). The following year, Harris portrayed Abbé Faria in *The Count of Monte Cristo*.

# Consider the Consequences

> *"The trouble is, humans do have a knack of choosing precisely those things that are worst for them."*
> —Albus Dumbledore, *Harry Potter and the Sorcerer's Stone*

Y ou'd be hard-pressed to find someone who doesn't think they know what's best for themselves. And when you've got as ambitious a plan as achieving immortality, like Voldemort, you probably won't contemplate Murphy's Law and envision the ways your scheme could derail or the harm it could cause. You may even finally grasp the thing you've wanted only for others to have to talk sense into you, as when Ron and Dumbledore dissuade Harry from gazing at the parents he never knew in the Mirror of Erised. Power corrupts no matter how noble your initial intentions. Before you commit to an objective, consider who and what you could lose if you get more than you bargain for.

Matthew Lewis as Neville Longbottom and Daniel Radcliffe as Harry Potter in *Harry Potter and the Sorcerer's Stone* (2001). Lewis began acting at the age of 5 and made his debut in a 1996 episode of the crime drama *Dalziel and Pascoe*.

# Find Your Voice and Use It

Sticking to your convictions takes gumption.

Assertiveness doesn't come naturally to everyone, especially those who grew up under the colossal weight of others' achievements. Such is the case with Neville Longbottom. Effectively orphaned, Neville is raised by a strict and overbearing grandmother who constantly measures him against the heroic exploits of his parents, allies of Dumbledore whom Bellatrix Lestrange tortured to insanity. It's a burdensome legacy, and from the day he meets Severus Snape and Draco Malfoy, Neville is consistently reminded of the many reasons he is a disappointment.

During his first year, despite having yet to find the strength to properly stand up for himself, when Neville discovers Harry, Ron and Hermione sneaking out of bed one night, he takes Ron's advice and insists they abandon their plan. And even though he cites not wanting to cost Gryffindor any more House points as the reason, it's the first time we see Neville stick to his morals in the face of opposition. Once Neville manages to stand up to the trio, he's got the momentum that ultimately takes him from confronting a Snape-shaped boggart to joining Harry in the Department of Mysteries to leading the Death Eater resistance at Hogwarts and ultimately opposing Voldemort face-to-face.

It may take practice and a little trial and error just like it did for Neville, but you'll find your voice in time. Others are counting on it.

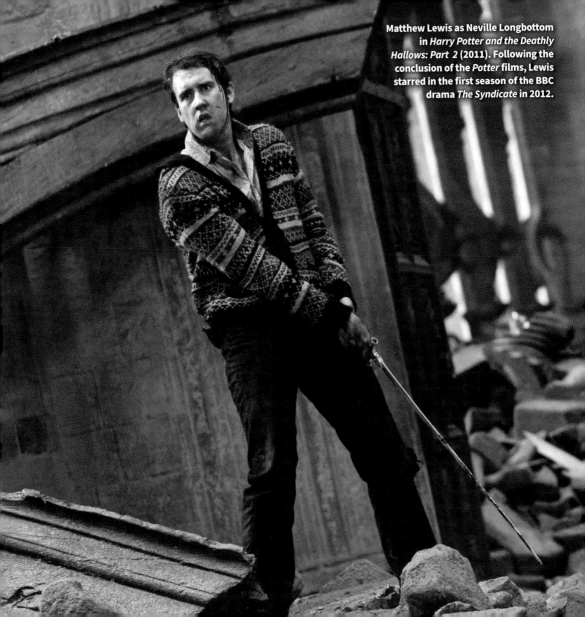

Matthew Lewis as Neville Longbottom in *Harry Potter and the Deathly Hallows: Part 2* (2011). Following the conclusion of the *Potter* films, Lewis starred in the first season of the BBC drama *The Syndicate* in 2012.

> *"The thing about growing up with Fred and George is that you sort of start thinking anything's possible if you've got enough nerve."*
> —GINNY WEASLEY,
> *Harry Potter and the Half-Blood Prince*

When Harry is troubled by discovering the sort of teenagers his father and godfather had been, the youngest Weasley sibling encourages him to reach out to Sirius. Sure, Umbridge has ramped up security at the school, but as Ginny's tenacious twin brothers have taught her, where there's a will, there's a clever workaround. With a little creativity, there's no telling what you can accomplish.

James Phelps, Bonnie Wright, Oliver Phelps and Rupert Grint in *Harry Potter and the Order of the Phoenix* (2007).

Emma Watson, Daniel Radcliffe and Rupert Grint as Hermione, Harry and Ron in *Harry Potter and the Sorcerer's Stone* (2001). The *Harry Potter* series has been translated into more than 80 languages.

# It Takes a Hogsmeade

## Not even the most rugged individualist can escape the people and places that shaped them.

It isn't a stretch to say Harry owes his life to the magical community. Whether it's the Order of the Phoenix, which mobilized to bring him safely to Number Four, Privet Drive the night his parents were murdered, or the leaders at Hogwarts, who provided him with a means to channel his magical abilities and thrive in wizarding society, it's clear Harry did nothing of his own accord to earn the title the Boy Who Lived. And he'd be the first to admit it.

No matter what successes or triumphs Harry faces in his seven years of schooling, he's quick to point out the circumstances that factored into the equation. Though it's not a stretch to say Harry was born humble, you could argue his humility was solidified by Dumbledore's first lesson, devised as far back as *Sorcerer's Stone*: There's practically zero chance Harry could've navigated the wizard chess game or selected the correct potion (let alone wriggled free of the Devil's Snare) without Ron and Hermione's input, even if he did snatch the Stone before it fell into Voldemort's hands. These intricate, complex protections were designed to test more than one first-year student, and as we see four books later, Harry's decidedly not in the business of telling lies. When his classmates recount his accomplishments, rather than smile and nod, he sheepishly admits how much help he'd received along the way.

It can be tempting to claim our success is due to how much natural talent or elbow grease we're willing to apply to any one thing. But you don't have to be a Gryffindor to see it takes a special blend of "daring, nerve and chivalry" to acknowledge those who lent their time and abilities to aid you in your journey.

Daniel Radcliffe, Rupert Grint and Emma Watson as Harry, Ron and Hermione in *Harry Potter and the Deathly Hallows: Part 2* (2011). The following year, Watson starred in *The Perks of Being a Wallflower*.

Rupert Grint in character as Ron in a promotional photo for *Harry Potter and the Chamber of Secrets* (2002). Grint also portrayed Ron in the final four *Harry Potter* video games.

# You're Only as Good as Your Tools

*"[Ron] had patched up his wand with some borrowed Spellotape, but it....kept crackling and sparking at odd moments..."*
—*Harry Potter and the Chamber of Secrets*

When it comes to material possessions, Ron has no say in anything from his robes to his pet rat to his hand-me-down wand. He breaks the latter while returning to Hogwarts, and for the rest of the year, the temperamental object refuses to work and even backfires. Sure, it saves Ron and Harry from being Obliviated, but only because it casts Gilderoy Lockhart's expert spell back at him—a close call of epic proportions—and it also earned him a mouth full of slugs. Fortunately, we don't have to cough up buckets of mollusks to learn this takeaway: The proper equipment won't automatically turn anyone into an expert in their field, but it can maximize whatever skills you possess. When you want the job done right, pick the right tool.

Daniel Radcliffe as Harry Potter in *Harry Potter and the Goblet of Fire* (2005). From 2007 to 2009, Radcliffe starred as Alan Strang in the West End and Broadway productions of *Equus*.

# You'll Never Walk Alone

No matter what challenges you may face, you can always call on the support of your loved ones to keep going.

I n a series where so much depends on Harry readying himself for the final showdown against Voldemort, it can be difficult to remember that at some point, Harry will have to enter that ultimate conflict alone, without any of the help upon which he can usually count. This is a far cry from the trials he went through protecting the Sorcerer's Stone: He can't count on Hermione to provide the deductive reasoning or for Ron to step in and fight on his behalf (not that he would ever ask them to do either). In order to fulfill the prophecy and ensure Voldemort meets his mortal end, this can only be a one-on-one duel. That's why it's so jarring when, during a ceasefire in the battle of Hogwarts, Harry accepts that he must die in order to best his enemy. And because no wizard in their right mind would allow him to make that sacrifice, he dons the Invisibility Cloak and slips away from his friends, teachers and classmates on a march to Voldemort's encampment, where he offers himself up to his enemy without so much as raising his wand.

As anyone who's ever had to face a challenge knows, sometimes you've got to do it on your own. But just as Harry calls on positive moments in his past to dispel Dementors and ready himself for the culmination of the Battle of Hogwarts, you can summon thoughts of your family, friends and other loved ones to keep going, no matter what lies ahead. The steadying power of knowing he was loved would have bolstered Harry in battle even without the Resurrection Stone, and you can count on the same kind of magic in your own life. As the *Harry Potter* saga makes clear, there's no more powerful kind of sorcery in the world.

There's little in this world short of a Memory Charm that can separate you from recollections that give you strength and hope. You don't even need a Pensieve.

Daniel Radcliffe and Ralph Fiennes as Harry Potter and Voldemort in *Harry Potter and the Deathly Hallows: Part 2* (2011). That year, Fiennes made his directorial debut in a film adaptation of Shakespeare's tragedy *Coriolanus*, in which he played the titular role.

Daniel Radcliffe as Harry Potter and Evanna Lynch as Luna Lovegood in *Harry Potter and the Order of the Phoenix* (2007).

*"Things we lose have a way of coming back to us in the end, if not always in the way we expect."*

—Luna Lovegood,
*Harry Potter and the Order of the Phoenix* (2007)

At the end of Harry's fifth year at Hogwarts, Luna shares with Harry—who's grieving Sirius's death—that people have been hiding her things. When he offers to help her look, she declines, then offers her late mother's advice with the above line. Like Harry, Luna's no stranger to loss, but there's hope: The people and things we cherish stay with us long after their physical forms are gone. Such feelings leave lasting impressions no degree of distance can undo. Not all that's lost is fully gone—you just might have to look more diligently to find it.

Robbie Coltrane as Rubeus Hagrid in *Harry Potter and the Goblet of Fire* (2005). In 2006, Queen Elizabeth II appointed him (along with fellow *Potter* cast member Imelda Staunton) as Officer of the Order of the British Empire (OBE) for his services to drama.

# There's No Use Worrying

*"No good sittin' worryin' abou' it. What's comin' will come, an' we'll meet it when it does."*
—Rubeus Hagrid, *Harry Potter and the Goblet of Fire*

In *Goblet of Fire*, the wizarding community is first informed Voldemort has returned. But even in the harshest moment he's yet seen, Hagrid refuses to give in to despair. He's not unprepared, he's simply more concerned with the things he can control, the most important of which is the attitude with which he approaches a challenge. Worrying about the future won't change what's coming. Even Harry—doomed to face off in a death struggle with the most powerful Dark wizard of all time—doesn't let that consume his thoughts. A healthy amount of concern for the challenges of the future keeps us honest and ready for a bump in the proverbial road. Getting too worked up about what's wrong or what might go awry prevents us from performing when the time comes. Be like Hagrid: Cross those bridges when you get to them.

David Thewlis as Remus Lupin in *Harry Potter and the Deathly Hallows: Part 1* (2010). The film received two Academy Award nominations: Best Art Direction and Best Visual Effects.

# We All Carry Trauma

The human experience is varied and wonderful.
Even pain can bring us together.

W e don't all carry equal amounts of trauma, but like our mistakes, our traumas can be a valuable wellspring of education for the future or a Dementor-like force, sucking the joy out of everything. If we unpack our emotional baggage—whether it's through journaling, psychotherapy or whatever helps you cope—empathy for the suffering of others becomes more meaningful and easier to come by. In the *Harry Potter* series, Remus Lupin refuses to do this, allowing the trauma from the violent origins of his lycanthropy, when Fenrir Greyback attacked him as a child, to burden him well into adulthood. Lupin's past weighs more heavily on him than anything else: It means that once a month, he's a threat to others. By not confronting his past, he allows that pain and stigma to isolate him, even from his own friends and family. Though he puts on a brave face, his stoic façade chips away when he lets people into his feelings.

As the Second Wizarding War rages on, Lupin finds a semblance of the things he's missed out on when the shape-shifting Nymphadora Tonks enters his life. But Lupin, for all the good he does in the world, is ill-equipped to let his newfound love bring him genuine peace. Instead, he continues to allow his trauma to define him, fixating on whether or not any child he might father could be born a werewolf rather than celebrating his new family. Lupin's plight is a reminder to lean on your inner circle of trusted loved ones and to resist the urge to isolate yourself. You are never a burden, and you're not alone. Loss, death, harm, error and regret come for us all, whether we're born into privilege or under the most humble circumstances. All the more reason to support one another.

David Thewlis as Remus Lupin in *Harry Potter and the Prisoner of Azkaban* (2004). In an interview with *Pick of the Flicks*, Thewlis explained he took inspiration for his performance from one of his former teachers.

**Michael Gambon as Albus Dumbledore in** *Harry Potter and the Half-Blood Prince* **(2009). That year, Gambon voiced Franklin Bean in** *Fantastic Mr. Fox*.

# Your Thoughts Create Your Reality

> *"Of course it is happening inside your head, Harry, but why on earth should that mean that it is not real?"*
> —ALBUS DUMBLEDORE, *Harry Potter and the Deathly Hallows*

As John Milton—another English author who understood the magical power of words and imagination—said, "The mind is its own place, and in itself can make a heaven of hell, a hell of heaven." In other words, just because you imagine something doesn't make the effect it has on you any less real. Every undertaking, from the largest infrastructure projects to the most concise short story, begins as a thought. The problem is it's easy to let our minds get away from us. We might not be able to break the laws of physics to solve problems like wizards, but we can certainly practice the Muggle equivalent of Occlumency by learning mindfulness techniques that help us keep calm and carry on or even boost our creativity. Discipline your mind, as Snape says, and there's no telling how much you can accomplish.

Michael Gambon as Albus Dumbledore and Daniel Radcliffe as Harry Potter in *Harry Potter and the Goblet of Fire* (2005).

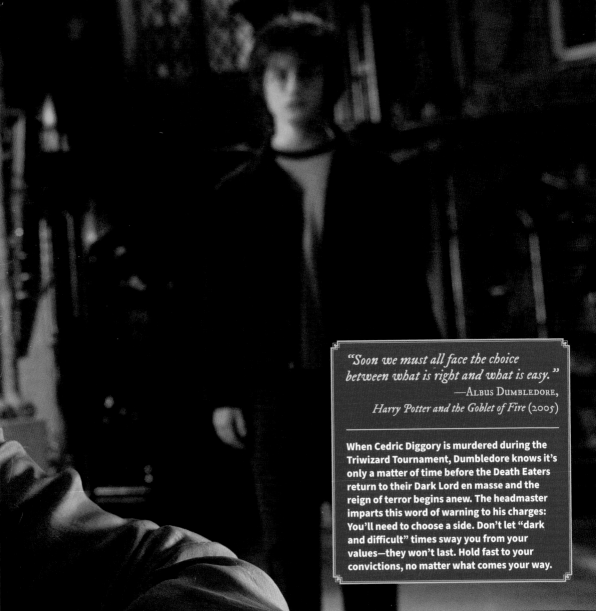

> *"Soon we must all face the choice
> between what is right and what is easy."*
> —ALBUS DUMBLEDORE,
> *Harry Potter and the Goblet of Fire* (2005)

---

When Cedric Diggory is murdered during the
Triwizard Tournament, Dumbledore knows it's
only a matter of time before the Death Eaters
return to their Dark Lord en masse and the
reign of terror begins anew. The headmaster
imparts this word of warning to his charges:
You'll need to choose a side. Don't let "dark
and difficult" times sway you from your
values—they won't last. Hold fast to your
convictions, no matter what comes your way.

Dobby the elf performs wandless magic in *Harry Potter and the Chamber of Secrets* (2002). Toby Jones voiced the character both times he appeared in the film series—in *Chamber of Secrets* and *Harry Potter and the Deathly Hallows: Part 1* (2010).

# Asking for Help Is Not a Sign of Weakness

### Harry, famously, is always reluctant to ask for aid. Don't make the same mistake.

T hroughout the *Harry Potter* series, from his foray into the forbidden third-floor corridor to his ill-fated after-hours journey to the Ministry of Magic, Harry has a tendency to act first and ask questions later. It's very Gryffindor of him, sure, but that doesn't make it a positive trait. Not only is Harry's proclivity for getting things done alone often mistaken for an overwhelming need for praise and attention, but it can prove dangerous, both to him and those who care about his well-being.

Consider this: If Harry hadn't had Dobby to help him with the second task of the Triwizard Tournament—Neville for you movie

ASKING FOR HELP IS NOT A SIGN OF WEAKNESS

buffs—he would have never been able to save Ron or Gabrielle Delacour. It's unlikely Dumbledore would have allowed the merpeople of the lake to cause the pair any harm in the second task, but it's this same need to go into the fray alone that later requires the Order of the Phoenix to rescue him from Voldemort's ambush at the Ministry of Magic. This daring mission costs Harry the only real family he's found to that point—his godfather, Sirius Black. If Harry hadn't rushed off in a hurry, he might have had time to consider whether or not his archenemy was leading him into a trap.

While the Boy Who Lived possesses numerous admirable traits, this is one it's best not to emulate. If you come across something that requires outside help, recognize that doing it alone could cause more harm than good. No matter how clever you are, you're not an expert in everything. When you're not in your element, defer to the experts and call on people you trust to help you get the job done.

Gary Oldman and Daniel Radcliffe in *Harry Potter and the Order of the Phoenix* (2007). Oldman reprised his role as Sirius Black in *Harry Potter and the Deathly Hallows: Part 2* (2011).

Ralph Fiennes as Voldemort in *Harry Potter and the Deathly Hallows: Part 2* (2011). According to Tom Felton, the scene in which Voldemort embraces Draco was improvised.

# Cut Out Toxic Friendships

> *"Your devotion is nothing more than cowardice.*
> *You would not be here if you had anywhere else to go."*
> —Lord Voldemort, *Harry Potter and the Goblet of Fire*

P eter Pettigrew, a man who betrayed his closest friends before spending 12 long years as a rat, cares only for self-preservation. As with any tyrant, the Dark Lord's paranoia means he distrusts virtually all of the people around him: When he isn't actively pursuing Harry, Voldemort busies himself by calculating the motivations of his supposed supporters. There's something to be gained from his choosy nature when it comes to letting anyone into your inner circle. Not everyone has your best interests at heart, and they might not be all they seem (Snape, anyone?). You certainly don't want to be in a position to depend on them, as when Voldemort mistakenly assumes Pettigrew will return to him in his hour of need. Don't hesitate to cut toxic people out of your life. Better to know they won't be there for you than to have your assumptions proved correct at the worst possible time.

Rupert Grint, Bonnie Wright, James Phelps and Oliver Phelps in *Harry Potter and the Order of the Phoenix* (2007). Wright made her directorial debut in 2012 with the short film *Separate We Come, Separate We Go.*

# Money Only Gets You So Much

**Funds might ease your troubles, but true wealth lies in having the support of friends and family.**

Anyone who's ever championed the claim that money can't buy happiness would likely get a mouthful from Ron Weasley. The second-youngest of seven siblings doesn't get so much as his own wand until he's 13 years old, two years after most of his classmates. Raised with hand-me-downs that saw better days several brothers before him, Ron knows his family pinches every Knut...and they're a Galleon short.

This may be why he's positively gobsmacked when his new friend Harry buys up the entire trolley of sweets on their first trip aboard the *Hogwarts Express* (something he's only able to do because his parents left him a tidy sum in a Gringotts vault). Never mind how Harry grew up with an aunt and uncle who loathe him and a cousin who regularly beats him up—for Ron, all that coin to spare means Harry could splurge on a gold cauldron if he wanted. This safety net occasionally blinds Harry to the needs of others—when Ron's secondhand wand breaks in their second year, Harry can't fathom why he won't write home for a new one. But for all of Ron's insecurity about his family's finances, he overlooks how the Weasleys are far richer than Harry ever will be: They're a large, happy family who genuinely enjoy each other's company, an ancient wizarding clan who make their way in the world with ingenuity, humor and hard work. And even when the budget barely accommodates textbooks, they provide for Harry as though he were a son.

Whether you're set like Harry or wish you had a few things of your own like Ron, remember the support of your loved ones is a safety net worth its weight in gold.

Rupert Grint as Ron Weasley in *Harry Potter and the Half-Blood Prince* (2009). As part of the 2012 Summer Olympics, Grint participated in the torch relay, carrying the Olympic flame through Hendon in London.

> *"It takes a great deal of bravery to stand up to our enemies, but just as much to stand up to our friends."*
> —Albus Dumbledore, *Harry Potter and the Sorcerer's Stone*

It's easy to want to confront an adversary and challenge them—you already look at them with a critical eye. But when those you care about are in the wrong, it can be that much more difficult to say what needs to be said for fear of turning them against you, as when Neville tells Harry, Ron and Hermione to stop sneaking out of the Gryffindor common room after curfew. The thing is, true friends know to speak up when someone is flirting with danger or putting others at risk.

Members of the
Hogwarts staff
in *Harry Potter
and the Sorcerer's
Stone* (2001).

Emma Watson as Hermione Granger in *Harry Potter and the Goblet of Fire* (2005). Watson starred as Meg March in the 2019 film adaptation of *Little Women*.

# Confront Injustice

No matter your background, you can
help make the world a better place.

Being born a wizard in a wizard's world is great: you grow up with family members who are well-versed in spellwork and de-gnoming gardens. You can identify what a Muggle is, even if you're discouraged from interacting with them. This is the environment in which Ron and Draco, both from pure-blood families, spend their formative years. Harry and Hermione, on the other hand, couldn't be more different. Raised by non-magical people, their default worldview is to rely on logic and labor to get things done. When the two arrive at Hogwarts, it's clear their peers are miles ahead of them as far as basic cultural knowledge is concerned (and part of why Hermione uses a Time-Turner to get up to speed). Her parentage also earns her a new insult: Mudblood.

But given that she's new to the magical community, Hermione hasn't been conditioned to accept things the way they are or take them for granted: When she discovers how cruelly elves are treated by the families they serve, she speaks up. By forming the Society for the Promotion of Elfish Welfare (S.P.E.W.), Hermione hopes to raise awareness of their status in society and champion their rights. Unfortunately, many students regard it as a joke, so the group never gains much traction. But in time, Hermione convinces some people—including Ron—to view elves who work in houses in a better light. It's a small step, but a step nonetheless.

Wherever you are, there are bound to be ways you can stand up for others. You might be mocked, and you may not succeed overnight, but even if you help one person change their worldview, you'll have made a difference.

Rupert Grint, Emma Watson and Daniel Radcliffe in *Harry Potter and the Prisoner of Azkaban* (2004). Both Emma Watson and her body double Flick Miles filmed the scene in which Hermione punches Draco, but according to Miles, Watson's superior punch made the final cut.

Michael Gambon as Albus Dumbledore in *Harry Potter and the Half-Blood Prince* (2009). Gambon made his film debut in *Othello* (1965) alongside Laurence Olivier and future *Potter* alum Maggie Smith.

# Have the Right Attitude

*"And now, Harry, let us step out into the night and pursue that flighty temptress, adventure."*
—ALBUS DUMBLEDORE, *Harry Potter and the Half-Blood Prince*

Whether you're a glass-half-full person or not, it's not pessimistic to admit how few things we can control. Harry has no say over his destiny (aside from the House into which he's Sorted), just as Dumbledore can't walk away from helping Harry—the world depends on it. But whether your goal entails mastering self-defense or avoiding the grossest Bertie Bott's Every Flavor Beans out there, each of us has a say in the attitude with which we choose to face life. With a typically lovely turn of phrase, the headmaster utters the above line prior to whisking Harry away on a rather mundane errand: convincing Horace Slughorn to resume his post at Hogwarts. It's tedious work cajoling someone out of retirement, but the Potions students aren't going to instruct themselves. Dumbledore could've just as breezily said this line while hunting Horcruxes. He embraces his duties—including the seemingly bland ones—with enthusiasm, and so should you.

Michael Gambon and Daniel Radcliffe in *Harry Potter and the Half-Blood Prince* (2009). Beginning in 2014, Gambon lent his voice to *The Elder Scrolls Online* video games.

# Empathy Changes Your Perspective

**Be willing to see things from someone else's point of view.**

N o one among us could say with any sincerity that they haven't wanted to get their hands on a Time-Turner. The desire to undo the past makes for potent, transformative magic. But since we have no chance of altering that which has already transpired, we must confront the ways in which we should change ourselves: to have more patience, speak with kindness or simply listen. Aiding this transfiguration of the soul, at least in Harry's world, is another enchanting object: the Pensieve, the basin into which any thought or memory can be poured, examined or relived, with all details and feelings preserved.

By utilizing this rare object, Harry witnesses Tom Riddle's metamorphosis into Lord Voldemort and Severus Snape's arc from bullied student (at the hands of Harry's father, no less) to repentant

Death Eater and double agent. No matter whose memories Harry probes, each visit underscores the same truth: No one is wholly good or evil—our choices define our character.

While no one knows the exact magical means by which Pensieves operate, we Muggles have access to it in the form of empathy. You need not immerse yourself in a tub of silvery, opaque liquid to step outside of your perspective (but by all means, use a bath bomb if it helps)—it can be as simple as reframing your mindset. By practicing mindfulness and considering what others are going through, we can embrace reacting with logic and compassion rather than out of anger or fear, the very things that spark regrettable moments in the first place. Short of time travel, self-reflection helps us uncover truths we might've missed, no wand required.

Emma Watson and Daniel Radcliffe in *Harry Potter and the Prisoner of Azkaban* (2004). Both actors divide their time between the U.S. and their native U.K.

> "I am what I am, an' I'm not ashamed. 'Never be ashamed,' my ol' dad used ter say, 'there's some who'll hold it against you, but they're not worth botherin' with.'"
>
> —RUBEUS HAGRID,
> *Harry Potter and the Goblet of Fire*

There's plenty of prejudice in the wizarding community, especially for a half-giant like Hagrid. He's never quite fit in among magic folk or giants. Unlike those who look down on him, Hagrid sees nothing wrong with his parentage: It defines his bone structure, sure, but little else. Take a note from Hagrid: You are far more than the biases with which others view you. Their opinions need not hold sway over your life.

Robbie Coltrane as Rubeus Hagrid and Daniel Radcliffe as Harry Potter in *Harry Potter and the Chamber of Secrets* (2002).

Evanna Lynch as Luna Lovegood in *Harry Potter and the Half-Blood Prince* (2009). She released her memoir, *The Opposite of Butterfly Hunting*, in 2021.

# Be Yourself, Unapologetically

To inhabit one's weirdness is to live authentically.
Don't mold yourself to fit others' expectations.

Coming into one's own can make for a lonely experience, especially at a school filled with adolescents learning to control their magic. To embrace your idiosyncrasies and speak your mind is not for the faint of heart. It's also part of what makes Luna Lovegood one of Harry's most admirable friends.

Called "Loony" by her detractors, the self-admittedly spacey Ravenclaw has just as much right to be at Hogwarts as Harry does—they're both wizards, after all—but where Harry seeks to adjust to magical society and take his place in it, Luna pays no mind to standing out like a Knarl among the hedgehogs (not that she craves the attention). Decked out in bizarre homemade jewelry and funky glasses and prone to chatting about imaginary creatures, she is decidedly not everyone's glass of butterbeer. But for all her eccentricities, Luna doesn't hesitate to call things as she sees them, just as when she assures Harry that she, too, can see the skeletal steeds pulling the Hogwarts carriages. By opening up about their respective losses, Luna and the Boy Who Lived form a lasting friendship. Bluntness aside, her empathy, intelligence and enthusiasm eventually endear her to her classmates.

Depending on your background, you may seek to please others, go with the flow or keep a low profile as you go about your day. None of these things is intrinsically bad, of course, but if doing so requires altering your values or minimizing the attributes that form the core of your being, you're doing yourself a disservice. Allow others the chance to see you exactly as you are. You never know what kindred spirits might be drawn to your light.

Evanna Lynch as Luna Lovegood in *Harry Potter and the Half-Blood Prince* (2009). An animal rights advocate, Lynch cofounded Kinder Beauty, a vegan cosmetics subscription box, in 2018.

**Daniel Radcliffe as Harry Potter and Chris Rankin as Percy Weasley in** *Harry Potter and the Order of the Phoenix* **(2007). Rankin's character appears in all but three of the** *Potter* **films:** *Harry Potter and the Goblet of Fire* **(2005),** *Harry Potter and the Half-Blood Prince* **(2009) and** *Harry Potter and the Deathly Hallows: Part 1* **(2010).**

# Admit When You're Wrong

*"Dumbledore says people find it far easier to forgive others for being wrong than being right."*
—HERMIONE GRANGER, *Harry Potter and the Half-Blood Prince*

Mistakes are a frequent if regrettable part of life. Still, to double down on a bad judgment call rather than make amends for being wrong often requires a swan dive into delusion. That's why it's so disheartening when Percy Weasley does just that, siding with the Ministry of Magic and denying Voldemort's return. He's a yes-man now, and climbing the ladder means toeing the line. But when Death Eaters take over the Ministry, Percy realizes he's become a complicit player in an evil regime. In the above quote, Hermione highlights Percy's unwillingness to reconcile with his family after allowing his ambition to steer him from making wise choices, as framed by Dumbledore's kind advice. When you know you're in the wrong, spare yourself (and others) heartache and face facts. You're not just admitting your mistakes to others—you're admitting them to yourself.

Daniel Radcliffe as Harry Potter in *Harry Potter and the Order of the Phoenix* (2007). Although the fifth book is the longest of the series (896 pages), its film adaptation is the second shortest of the series (beaten only by 2011's *Harry Potter and the Deathly Hollows: Part 2*).

# Growth Means Pushing Through Your Fears

## Avoiding something (or refusing to say its name) only gives it power over you.

The stakes at the heart of the *Potter* series are simple. Harry must duel Voldemort and eliminate the Dark wizard's reign of terror once and for all. But to accomplish that, he's got to do more than sharpen his skills and survive—Harry must repeatedly confront his mortality and that of his loved ones (per the prophecy, "neither can live while the other survives" leaves no convenient wiggle room for a crafty workaround). While Remus Lupin's lesson on banishing boggarts is one of the most effective lessons of Harry's schooling—successfully helping 13-year-olds tackle the things that frighten them has far-reaching benefits beyond banishing boggarts—it's one of many the series has to offer about the inherent liberating power of harnessing your fears rather than letting them control you.

The choice between pressing on despite your fears and allowing them to consume you shapes virtually all of magical society. It's the dividing line between those who want to see Harry triumph and those who serve the Dark Lord, the driving force between an act of sacrifice or self-preservation. Indeed, the Dark wizard's obsession with cheating death compels him to commit murder and split his soul time and time again. When he and his followers wreak havoc on wizards and Muggles alike, people outright avoid even referring to him by name, which only serves to magnify the scope of his power.

Whether you need to stare down a spider or accept that death comes for us all, growing as a person means pushing through your fears.

Daniel Radcliffe as Harry Potter and Ralph Fiennes as Voldemort in *Harry Potter and the Deathly Hallows: Part 1* (2010). Fiennes portrays Voldemort in two of the *Potter* video games: *Harry Potter and the Goblet of Fire* (2005) and *Harry Potter and the Order of the Phoenix* (2007).

> *"Fear of a name increases fear of the thing itself."*
>
> —Albus Dumbledore,
> *Harry Potter and the Sorcerer's Stone*

As early as the first book in the *Potter* series, Dumbledore instills a valuable lesson in Harry: Face your fears head on. One of the easiest ways to begin that is by naming that which scares you. The headmaster advises: "Always use the proper name." In other words, speak plainly and call a Dementor a Dementor. Otherwise, you risk not only preserving trauma but also magnifying it.

Rupert Grint, Emma Watson and Daniel Radcliffe in *Harry Potter and the Sorcerer's Stone* (2001). Watson and Radcliffe considered leaving the franchise after the fourth and third films, respectively.

# Hobbies
# Help Us Grow

Cultivating a skill can bring you joy and keep you well-rounded.

I t's easy to lose yourself in the grind. Whether you're taking so many classes you need a Time-Turner just to keep up or stockpiling Galleons in the bank, the tedium of day-to-day responsibilities and the endless march of boxes to be checked takes a toll. But wasting away at a keyboard is as preventable as wasting away in front of the Mirror of Erised. For anyone who doesn't have a plentiful vault at Gringotts to rely on, you can preserve your sanity by stealing a few moments each day to devote to a creative pursuit that brings you happiness.

For example, there's Ron, who arrives at Hogwarts with an extensive grasp of wizard chess. It's not taught in any class (which is likely why Hermione doesn't master it)—Ron simply brings his grandfather's old set with him to school for no other reason than that he enjoys playing the game. He never loses to Harry or Hermione, and his knack for strategy comes in handy when the friends discover they need to win a game of life-size chess to save the Sorcerer's Stone. His skills even prompt Dumbledore to award 50 points to Gryffindor, a prime accolade that sets Ron apart and helps him make a name for himself at the school.

Could Ron have foreseen how wizard chess would make him a hero? He certainly didn't see it in the Mirror of Erised. But there's no denying the patience and tenacity required to master the game bolstered his confidence and gave him a sense of identity at a time when he needed it most (and with high-achieving friends like Hermione and Harry, Ron would like his place in the sun once in a while, too). The lesson? Finding an outlet for your talents can pay dividends in ways you can hardly dream.

Emma Watson, Rupert Grint and Daniel Radcliffe in *Harry Potter and the Sorcerer's Stone* (2001). The chess pieces in this scene are inspired by the Lewis Chessmen, 12th-century chess pieces recovered on a beach in Scotland in 1831.

Robbie Coltrane as Rubeus Hagrid in *Harry Potter and the Order of the Phoenix* (2007). Coltrane first took up acting while attending Glenalmond College, a boarding school in Scotland.

# You Are More Than Your Job

*"There's things more importan' than keepin' a job."*
—Rubeus Hagrid, *Harry Potter and the Order of the Phoenix*

E ven when there's a war going on, some things take precedence over taking a paycheck, a lesson Hagrid teaches readers during Harry's fifth year at Hogwarts. As students and staff resist the tyrannical regime of Dolores Umbridge—whose ego and need for obedience are exceeded only by her hatred of half-bloods—Hagrid has been tasked with convincing the giants to form an alliance against Voldemort. Along the way, the gamekeeper discovers he has a half-brother, a giant whom Hagrid realizes is bullied by his tribe. Grawp, as he's called, takes priority over everything—he's the only family Hagrid has. When Harry cautions Hagrid to keep a low profile so as not to provoke Umbridge's wrath, the proud half-giant replies with the above line. Voldemort will have to wait, and the draconian headmistress ranks among the least of Hagrid's worries. Ultimately, even a job you've always wanted is replaceable. Your loved ones are not. Cherish them while you can.

Daniel Radcliffe as Harry Potter in *Harry Potter and the Sorcerer's Stone* (2001). Harry's feathered companion was portrayed by a number of snowy owls named Bandit, Elmo, Gizmo, Kasper, Oh Oh, Oops and Swoops.

# Life Is Better With Pets

### Creatures great and small can enrich your life and vice versa.

Unconditional love is a form of unparalleled magic, and there's no denying that some of its most powerful spellcasters number among those in the animal kingdom. Considering Harry spends 10 years of his childhood with people who can't stand him, having a pet doesn't just warm his spirits with snuggly affection—it preserves his sanity.

Hedwig, Harry's snowy owl given to him by Hagrid as a birthday gift, is the first friend the Boy Who Lived ever has (no, the spiders in his cupboard under the stairs don't count). She eases his loneliness while he waits out his days with the Dursleys at number four, Privet Drive, and her presence reminds Harry the magical world is not something he dreamt up—it's as real as she is.

But Hedwig's hardly the only pet who transforms their human's life. Hermione's fluffy ginger cat (well, half-Kneazle) Crookshanks doesn't just provide loyal companionship—he goes so far as to throw himself onto an innocent man whom Harry intends to murder, a selfless act by which he saves Sirius Black's life. An excellent judge of character, Crookshanks spends most of the trio's third year attempting to catch one sinister rat: Peter Pettigrew in Animagus form. Had Ron let him finish the job, it's difficult to say how Voldemort's return could've played out.

Even the Dark wizard himself, though incapable of love in its truest sense, displays an intense possessiveness toward his massive snake, Nagini. Granted, the *Fantastic Beasts* films also reveal there's more to this serpent than initially assumed, something to be mindful of the next time your own pet gazes at you with an almost human-like expression.

From Filch's other half, Mrs. Norris, to Hagrid's beloved boarhound Fang (not to mention the rest of his monstrous menagerie), no matter your alignment, a well-cared-for pet can flesh out the story of your life just as much as you shape theirs.

Emma Watson as Hermione Granger in *Harry Potter and the Prisoner of Azkaban* (2004). Hermione's pet, Crookshanks, was played by a Persian cat named Crackerjack.

> *"Love as powerful as your mother's for you leaves its own mark. To have been loved so deeply, even though the person who loved us is gone, will give us some protection forever."*
>
> —ALBUS DUMBLEDORE,
> *Harry Potter and the Sorcerer's Stone*

---

Lily Potter's love for her son does more than protect Harry when Voldemort tries to kill him—it's a fact that Harry can draw on like a Patronus Charm should the trauma of his childhood or feelings of persistent loneliness ever prove overwhelming. He was born to people who adored him, something his enemy will never understand. To have ever felt that support shapes our lives in ways we can hardly fathom. Don't take it for granted.

Richard Harris as Albus Dumbledore and Maggie Smith as Minerva McGonagall in *Harry Potter and the Sorcerer's Stone* (2001).

Daniel Radcliffe as Harry Potter and Gary Oldman as Sirius Black in *Harry Potter and the Order of the Phoenix* (2007). In a 2021 interview on *The Late Show with Stephen Colbert*, Radcliffe described Oldman as the first *Potter* cast member he felt "starstruck" around.

# Death Is Another Part of Life

### Remembering that every story has an end can remind you to seize the moment.

Various religions and philosophies have all taken a stab at confronting the impermanence of things, with arguably mixed results. An inability to accept how every life draws to a close can lead to prolonging the inevitable in increasingly ludicrous or harmful ways. Voldemort, a wizard whose talents rival Albus Dumbledore's (and whose chosen name contains the French word for death), commits his talents to spreading the thing he fears most in the name of achieving immortality. Because he dreads death, he never truly lives.

Beginning on the night Voldemort sets out to kill the Potters, the shadow of death looms over every aspect of Harry Potter's life. He bears a constant reminder of this: a lightning-bolt-shaped scar etched into his forehead, denoting his destiny to all who look at him. After Voldemort's followers return, Harry witnesses his classmate's murder and loses his godfather, mentor, feathered companion, elf friend and others within the span of three years. He isn't given much time or space to process their absence—instead, he must press on with his training for the final battle. But like a Remembrall that points to the eternal realm, Harry's memories of his loved ones signal how much there's still worth fighting for. And if Nearly Headless Nick is any indication, fearing what comes for us all doesn't make for the most fulfilling afterlife.

We each have a say in what we permit to haunt us. You can choose to banish the specter of your mortality to the periphery of your waking hours, secreting away those thoughts into a Shrieking Shack of denial. Or, you can look anew at your loved ones and passions and savor each moment you're given.

Robert Pattinson as Cedric Diggory in *Harry Potter and the Goblet of Fire* (2005). Pattinson made his film debut in *Vanity Fair* (2004), but his scene was deleted from the final cut.

Emma Watson as Hermione Granger in *Harry Potter and the Deathly Hallows: Part 1* (2010). Taking her character to heart, Watson suggested the film's set designers add more books to Hermione's bedroom.

# Remember the Bigger Picture

> *"I'm hoping to do some good in the world!"*
> —HERMIONE GRANGER, *Harry Potter and the Deathly Hallows*

Minister of Magic Rufus Scrimgeour is a battle-hardened Auror tasked with the impossible: taking down Lord Voldemort and his murderous cult of followers. Scrimgeour's methods are questionable at best; he often resorts to bending the rules. As an example, he withholds Dumbledore's belongings from the trio, hoping to uncover a plot by the late headmaster in the process. Hermione sees right through this and calls him on it. Taken on its own, the above quote brims with optimism—and it should, considering the bright future ahead of her. But within this scene, Hermione takes a stand: She rejects compromising one's ethics to ensure victory. No matter what you seek to accomplish, you'll wonder if the road you travel makes any difference (as one No-Maj poet opined). Don't let a difficult path tempt you to take a morally dubious shortcut. If you make a wrong turn, correct it posthaste—otherwise, you could lose yourself along the way.

Emma Watson, Rupert Grint, Alan Rickman and Daniel Radcliffe in *Harry Potter and the Prisoner of Azkaban* (2004), the only Potter installment directed by Alfonso Cuarón. Ten years later, Cuarón took home the 2014 Oscar for Best Director for *Gravity* (2013).

# Choose Kindness

**A single act can reverberate across someone's
day or echo for the rest of their life.**

I n the years since *Harry Potter and the Deathly Hallows* hit shelves,
much has been made about the revelation that Severus Snape was
not only childhood friends with Harry's mother—he loved her.
Determined to carry out Dumbledore's orders with his dying breath,
the acerbic Potions Master draws on the memories of his friend for
strength and resolve, as well as the occasional sobering reminder
of his debt to her. Regardless of whether this platonic relationship
hearkens back to courtly love or stems from a place of deluded
obsession, one thing is clear: Lily's kindness changed Snape for good.

Lily Evans befriends Snape when he's nothing more than a neglected,
lonely only child living in a house with an abusive father (it's entirely
possible she's the first person to show him kindness and warmth.) They

bond over their shared otherness as individuals with magical abilities, and he introduces her to the wizarding community she'll soon join. But even after they're Sorted into opposing Houses and begin to grow apart, Lily pointedly demonstrates her affection by confronting Snape when he falls in with, to use Draco's words, the "wrong sort": a gaggle of Death Eaters. Sadly, his anti-Muggle prejudice precludes him from heeding her caution until it is far too late.

Arguably the most complicated character in the series, Snape embraces a host of Gryffindor values once he channels his feelings for Lily into protecting others. You don't need those stakes to know every action counts. It goes to show that much as a candle is not dimmed by sharing its flame, an act of kindness can kindle goodness across countless lives (a long-lasting *Lumos* invisible to the eye, if you will).

Alan Rickman as Severus Snape in a publicity photo for *Harry Potter and the Order of the Phoenix* (2007). In 2022, Rickman's colorful private musings were published as *Madly, Deeply: The Diaries of Alan Rickman*.

Michael Gambon as Albus Dumbledore in *Harry Potter and the Deathly Hallows: Part 1* (2010).

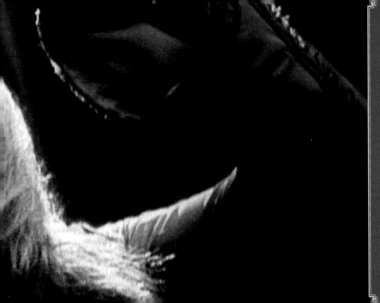

> *"Do not pity the dead, Harry. Pity the living, and above all, those who live without love."*
>
> —ALBUS DUMBLEDORE,
> *Harry Potter and the Deathly Hallows*

Given that he has a good heart, Harry can't help but feel compassion for his greatest adversary when he comes face-to-face with what Voldemort has become during the Battle of Hogwarts. Appearing to Harry in a sort of limbo state, Dumbledore redirects Harry's sentiments to the people who still have a chance to change—his friends and loved ones waiting for him among the living. There's power in the present; don't linger on what has already transpired.

# Live for the Present

## The only moment over which you have any direct influence is now.

The walking embodiment of wisdom in the wizarding world, Albus Dumbledore always keeps a few cards close to the vest (well, robe). When he finds Harry gazing at the Mirror of Erised in *Harry Potter and the Sorcerer's Stone* (2001), Dumbledore warns, "It does not do to dwell on dreams, Harry, and forget to live." What Harry (and, by extension, readers) can't possibly know is the extent to which this lesson shapes Dumbledore's life because he learned it the hard way.

The Mirror doesn't number among the Deathly Hallows, but that doesn't mean it isn't incredibly powerful—or dangerous. Like the Resurrection Stone, it is capable of producing the image of someone's loved one(s) so long as the gazer continues to look at it. Therein lies the threat, and as the headmaster explains, "Men have wasted away before it, entranced by what they have seen, or been driven mad." When Harry asks Dumbledore what he sees, the headmaster conceals that he shares Harry's desire: to see his family whole again. Decades after his mother's and sister's deaths (the latter of which occurred in a three-way duel with him, his brother and the Dark wizard Gellert Grindelwald), Dumbledore's grief remains unresolved. It's what compels him to challenge Dark magic at all costs, eventually by readying Harry to take on Voldemort.

Like Dumbledore, you may feel burdened with regret for your actions or inaction. But ruminating on the past only steals away from your ability to better the present. You may never undo the source of your grief, but you can honor it by having the courage to shape your life through forging a new path. That starts with prying yourself away from what could've been and focusing on what you have the power to change.

Daniel Radcliffe as Harry Potter and Michael Gambon as Albus Dumbledore in *Harry Potter and the Half-Blood Prince* (2009). The film was the first in the *Potter* series to mention Defense Against the Dark Arts without directly or indirectly depicting the course, when Dumbledore announces Severus Snape will teach the class.

Daniel Radcliffe as Harry Potter, Rupert Grint as Ron Weasley and Emma Watson as Hermione Granger in *Harry Potter and the Half-Blood Prince* (2009), which was the only *Potter* film to receive an Academy Award nomination for Best Cinematography.

# Stick Around

*"We're with you whatever happens."*
—RON WEASLEY, *Harry Potter and the Half-Blood Prince*

I t would've been dreadfully anticlimactic during the final book in the *Potter* series if Ron, pushed to his limits, abandoned his best friends in the middle of the Horcrux hunt and never returned. (Would Harry have drowned in the frozen pond? Who else would've rescued him in time?) Of course, Ron offers the above line in the penultimate book in the series—before he knows exactly how simultaneously tedious and dangerous things will get during their prolonged camping trip away from Hogwarts. But it's this spirit that compels Ron and Hermione to support their friend no matter what comes. Better to honor your commitments and finish what you start than to quit when the finish line is in sight.

Tom Felton as Draco Malfoy in *Harry Potter and the Half-Blood Prince* (2009). In 2022, Felton published a memoir, *Beyond the Wand: The Magic and Mayhem of Growing Up a Wizard.*

# Everyone Is the Hero of Their Own Story

## You are far from the only protagonist out there. That's a good thing.

The penultimate book of the *Potter* series does more than kill off Harry's beloved headmaster, Albus Dumbledore. It explores how a young man dehumanized himself to become the Dark wizard Voldemort. It's also a year in which Harry discovers the people he most despises—Voldemort, Snape and Draco—are just as human as he is. This realization doesn't just cement Harry's alignment to Dumbledore's cause—it makes him a better person.

By the time Harry's standing over a grievously injured Draco during a duel in *Half-Blood Prince*, two of the aforementioned lives are sealed: Neither Voldemort nor Snape has the power to undo the damage they caused during their early years. While Harry spends the year contemplating a career as an Auror, Draco completes a carpentry apprenticeship of sorts, repairing magical cabinets through which Death Eaters invade the school. When six years of rivalry come to a head and Harry tosses out an unknown curse he gleaned from a textbook, readers face an uncomfortable truth: Harry is bold (read: foolish) enough to use Dark magic. And when Draco, Harry's Slytherin counterpart, fails in his mission to kill Dumbledore, we see a glimmer of hope that perhaps Draco doesn't wish to follow in his father's footsteps. These young men whose lives reflect each other in myriad ways can stray from their chosen paths. They'll never look at each other in the same light again, a critical victory in the fight against the Dark Lord.

No one can fault you for getting caught up in the adventures of your own life—after all, you're only living the one. But remembering how people don't fit neatly into the Houses in which we readily Sort them can broaden our understanding of how all journeys progress one step at a time, including your own. Tread carefully.

Daniel Radcliffe as Harry Potter in *Harry Potter and the Half-Blood Prince* (2009). In 2022, in a departure from portraying a hero for a decade, Radcliffe won the MTV Movie Award for Best Villain for his role in *The Lost City*.

Alan Rickman as Severus Snape in *Harry Potter and the Deathly Hallows: Part 2* (2011).

*"After all this time?"*
*"Always," said Snape.*
—*Harry Potter and the Deathly Hallows*

The most iconic line in the *Potter* series (next to "Yer a wizard," anyway) is an affirmation of love. Snape's bisyllabic ode to the lasting power of one person's kindness, even after many years, encapsulates the force that drives Harry's saga: So long as we project it outward, love can fundamentally change us for the better. It does far more to render someone immortal than Horcruxes ever will. With one word, Snape taught us how to "stopper death" after all.

# Photo Credits

# Acknowledgments

To Jeff Ashworth, Tim Baker, Glen Karpowich, Courtney Kerrigan, Madeline Raynor, Phil Sexton and the rest of the team at Media Lab Books, your expertise, patience and humor shaped this title into something in which I take great pride. I am grateful for your hard work.

To my family, thank you for indulging my love of *Harry Potter* at a young age and allowing it to be a bright spot during my childhood.

Finally, to my husband, your unwavering support and eagerness to discuss *Potter* character development, plot points and hilarious lines at any hour, day or night, made writing this book feel like an adventure. After all this time, you're still my always.*

*Yes, that lone word was our wedding cake topper.

**JULIANA SHARAF** is a writer, editor and *Harry Potter* enthusiast whose past credits include *Everything I Need to Know I Learned from Betty White*, *Everything I Need to Know I Learned from Dolly Parton*, *John Wayne's Book of American Grit* and many more. She is also the lead editor of MuggleNet's bestselling *Unofficial Harry Potter Reference Library*. When she isn't penning or planning projects for Media Lab Books or serving potent potions to family and friends, she enjoys perfecting French desserts and mainlining espresso. She and her husband live in Florida with their dog, Brisket.

**Media Lab Books**
**For inquiries, call 646-449-8614**

Copyright 2023 Topix Media Lab

Published by Topix Media Lab
14 Wall Street, Suite 3C
New York, NY 10005

Printed in China

ISBN-13: 978-1-956403-27-5
ISBN-10: 1-956403-27-2